Hope in My Heart

Sofia's Immigrant Diary

· Book One ·

by Kathryn Lasky

Scholastic Inc. New York

The *Florida*
1903

January 30, 1903
Onboard the steamship *Florida*

Sometimes I think that what coming to America really means is choosing — choosing between bad choices and worse. For example, would I prefer to sleep in the bunk beneath the lady who smells like rotten fruit or the one who sleeps with the salami — a *soppressata*, the smelliest of all salamis? There is no escaping these smells. We must all sleep so close. We are packed into dark cabins like anchovies in a tin. We sleep in narrow bunks stacked three high.

My sister, Gabriella, says we probably smell,

too, because there are no showers. I say, not like a salami, I don't. So here is the next choice: no showers, or go on deck when it's raining and get pneumonia?

Oh, I could make such a long list. And we are only two weeks out from Genoa, Italy. "Only," they say! It seems like two years. And we have *only* maybe one more week — maybe — until we reach New York. Then add another year for the one week, and six months for the maybe. For that is what it will feel like. We, our family, the Monaris, are six in all. There is myself, Sofia. I am nine. There is my older sister, Gabriella, who is thirteen, and our two younger brothers: Luca is seven and baby Marco is eight months. Then there is our Mama and Papa.

We all come from Italy, the town of Cento. It is where the most beautiful, juiciest, tastiest tomatoes in Italy grow — in the world —

Papa says. But since my grandparents died, the Monari farm has gone to my father's oldest brother. That is the custom. So we decided to come to America where there are not so many customs, Papa says. Where it does not matter if you are the oldest or the youngest, but just how hard you work. I am not sure what work Papa will do. He talks of starting a grocery store.

January 31, 1903

The weather has turned rough again and Gabriella is throwing up. I am proud to say that I have not once thrown up on this trip. Papa says I have *un stommaco di ferro*, a stomach made of iron. I threw up once when I was four years old. I have not forgotten. I have a long memory. Do you know the famous volcano in Italy, Mount Vesuvius? It destroyed two whole cities, Pompei and Herculaneum.

Well, when I threw up, that is what it felt like. Vesuvius in my gut. *No grazie.* I am not a city waiting to be destroyed by an exploding volcano. I am a girl waiting to get to America. And the wait is long. It is boring and it is smelly.

February 1, 1903

Poor Gabriella! She was throwing up again today in the special throw-up bucket that Mama found somewhere and made it ours (our first new possession on our voyage to the land they call The Golden Country — how charming, I think, a throw-up bucket!). Anyhow, Signora Salami came over to Gabriella and began patting her head and leaning over her to comfort her. Of course with all that salami smell it made Gabriella throw up all the more. Imagine the ship tossing like crazy and then Signora Salami breathing in her face.

And do you know what Gabriella said after the lady left? "I think I'd rather be a nun than throw up one more time." See what I mean about choices? Great Auntie Mirella, Mama's aunt, is a nun at the convent of Santa Giustina dei Monti. Auntie wanted Gabriella to become a nun. But Gabriella didn't want to. I try to comfort Gabriella. I say "No, Gabi. You don't want to be a nun. It lasts longer than throwing up." I don't think she looks convinced. So I say, "You would not make a good nun." And she looks up slyly at me and says, "But I am a fantastic barfer!" And we both laugh. It is the first time I have seen her laugh in days. This must be a good sign.

February 2, 1903

The sea has smoothed out and the sun is out. Gabriella, Luca, and I go on deck with Papa. I squint hard into the horizon line. I try to imagine what this new country, this city with tall, tall buildings, will look like. Cento, where we lived, was a small city — well, not really a city, but bigger than a village. And all around the outside of the city were fields for growing tomatoes, and grapes for wine. "Papa," I say suddenly. "Do they grow tomatoes in New York City?"

"Oh no, there is not enough space."

"But what is there space for?" I ask.

"People, buildings, carts, uh . . . uh."

"But what do the people and the carts do?"

"Business."

Then Gabriella tells me I ask too many questions. But I have one last question. "If they don't grow tomatoes in the city, where do they grow them?"

"Out in the country," he replies.

This, of course, sets off Luca. "Out West with the cowboys and the Indians!" Luca is obsessed with cowboys and Indians. He wishes we were going out West instead of New York City. But I don't think they grow tomatoes out West. I don't think cowboys are interested in growing tomatoes. If they were, they would be called "tomato boys" and not "cowboys."

I suddenly miss tomatoes so fiercely that I can taste them. I swallow and think of Mama's *salsa pomodoro*, tomato sauce, and I think of tomato slices with basil in the summer. I think of tomatoes stuffed with rice. The sun is just beginning to set. It is sinking toward the horizon and just as it touches it begins to sort of squash out at the bottom where it meets the water. And you know what I picture? A big, red, juicy tomato. What kind of country can it be if it doesn't grow tomatoes?

February 3, 1903

They say that the first thing we will see of America is the Statue of Liberty. I cannot imagine what this statue might look like. She is supposed to stand very tall and carry a torch.

Later

There is this boy, Giuseppe. I think he likes Gabriella. He is fourteen and he is short, but he has a very nice face. Anyway, he is also very smart. He knows all about the Statue of Liberty. They call her Miss Liberty, he says. He drew us a picture of her. She wears a crown and holds a torch in one hand, and Giuseppe says that if you measure her from her feet to the tip of the torch she stands more than three hundred feet tall! But that is not the only amazing thing. Her hand is sixteen feet long and her finger is eight feet long. And guess how long her nose is? Four feet and six inches! They say we should begin looking for her in three days. But if the weather is good, Gabriella, Giuseppe, and I are going to start looking tomorrow.

February 4, 1903

No Miss Liberty yet. But I had a funny dream last night. I dreamed that there was a tomato stuck on the tip of that torch she carries.

Later

Still no Miss Liberty. But guess what? I saw that Gabriella and Giuseppe were holding hands! They didn't think anyone saw them because we were in a bunch of people on deck, all pressed together and looking out across the ocean. This is when it pays to be short. No view across the ocean, but a very good view of people's butts, old men's paunches, and people's hands. I saw you-know-who's hands. They had their fingers laced together — ever so casually. As a matter of fact, it made me think they had done this before. I am now wondering whether I should tell Gabriella what I saw. Probably not, but I'm not sure if I can resist. But if I do tell her they might stop doing it, or, worse, try to get away from me so they could hold hands. Then I would feel left out. I *hate* feeling left out.

Still later

They were doing it again this evening! I hope Gabriella realizes how right I was about her not being a good nun. Now let's hope she does not show her skills as a barfer. Oh my goodness, I would simply die of embarrassment if she threw up on Giuseppe.

February 5, 1903

Still no Miss Liberty. Still lots of hand-holding. No throwing up. I pray for calm seas for Gabriella's sake. If it does get rough, should I stand nearby with the throw-up bucket? I could hide it under my cape.

Later

I cannot believe it! Guess what? Giuseppe's aunt is Signora Salami! This is so embarrassing. He even says so. He says she loves soppressata and they begged her not to carry it all this way. He says, though, that she eats so much of it that even when she is not carrying it she still smells like it. He says in the summertime she sweats garlic! Maybe Gabriella should think twice about *really* falling in love with Giuseppe.

Still later

I have thought of one good thing about Giuseppe having Signora Salami as his aunt. If Gabriella throws up, well, she is not the only one who has something to be embarrassed about. So does Giuseppe. It's more even this way.

February 6, 1903

We see her! We see her! Miss Liberty at last. At first she was just a little smudge on the horizon. And then it was as if a very prickly star were melting out of the sky. That was her crown! The rays of the crown became clearer and clearer. Giuseppe says there are seven rays and these stand for the seven seas and the seven continents of the earth. He says this while secretly, so he thinks, holding Gabriella's hand, and Gabriella looks moony at him, as if he has just said the most impossibly romantic thing in the whole wide world.

I had a good view of Miss Liberty for about eight minutes. Then this incredibly fat man waddled in front of me. He was so rude and a fight broke out. I could have gotten squashed! I could have gotten trampled, maybe even tossed overboard in the fray! I was so mad. It's miserable being short. There are 1,600 people on this boat, and it seemed like every one of them were in front of me. I squirreled around and finally found a look-through place. Miss Liberty grows clearer with each minute that passes. I can see her torch now. Papa promises me that when we get really near, he will put me on his shoulders to see. I heard one of the crew say that it would be hours before we are really close. I hope it isn't dark by then.

Later

Even though it has started to rain slightly, people are bringing their blankets up on deck. They don't want to miss a thing. They will sleep out, no matter the weather, to see Miss Liberty.

A bit later

People are grumbling because, although the rain has lightened, the mist has thickened. They fear fog will hide Miss Liberty.

This fog might turn out to be a good thing for me, however. Papa has made friends with one of the sailors, who is in charge of the fog bell. He says that there is room for me near the bell where I can see a little more and still be protected from the crush of people on deck. There is a little niche right beneath where the bell is hung. It is perfect! The sailor's name is Franco. He is a jolly sort and he laughs when he sees me curl into the space. He calls it *la campenella di Sofia.* That means "the bell tower of Sofia." It's not really a tower, but it is raised a bit and I can see enough for now. And at least I am protected from being squashed by rude fat men. But Papa promises to come when we get closer and perch me even higher on his shoulders.

Oh my word, I fell asleep and suddenly I felt my whole head pounding! At first I didn't know what had happened, but soon I realized that Franco had rung the fog bell. I think it might have rattled my brains! I shall try to do some multiplication tables in my head — just to check.

Later

I did the nines tables perfectly, and they are the hardest. So I guess I am not brain damaged, and the fog is lifting. Soon, Franco says, he will tell me to fetch Papa.

February 7, 1903
Ellis Island

Quick! Hurry up! Run! These are my first English words. For that is all the officials, the inspectors, bark at you, from the ferryboat to the pier, and now into this building on Ellis Island. The island is across from another island, Manhattan. Manhattan, where the biggest city in the world is. New York. We arrived last night, and after we anchored in the harbor, a ferryboat came for us this morning.

Later

Stop! This is my new English word. No more *Hurry up!* No more *Quick!* This is the word that has been stitched in my mind, in my heart with ugly spidery black thread. My nightmare has begun. It began two hours ago when I was stopped by the inspectors. It is a long story but now I have plenty of time to write. You see, I am in "quarantine." I am separated from Mama and Papa and Luca and Gabriella and Marco. *Quarantena.* I had never even heard the word in Italian but now I am living it in English, in America. It means to separate because they fear I might spread disease. And what is this disease? Trachoma. Another word I had never heard of. This makes no sense. And yet the one word that would explain it all is the Italian word *"brace."* But I do not know how to say this word in English.

Now they take me to the hospital. It is on the second island that connects to Ellis Island. It is for people like me. Quarantine people. I cry "Mama," and I still hear her screaming at the Golden Door. That is what they call the last door immigrants pass through after they have been cleared for entry. Mama was cleared. Papa was cleared, Marco and Gabriella and Luca were cleared. But not me. The Golden Door slammed shut in my face and all I can hear is Mama wailing, screaming, screeching to God and Jesus.

February 8, 1903

I hate the Statue of Liberty! "Miss Liberty," they call her. Because of Miss Liberty I slept in a baby crib last night. That was the only bed they had because the hospital is so stuffed with people. A withered old man slept in a crib next to mine. He sucks his thumb and cries. I think he is of a feeble mind. They took the end of the crib off for him so his feet can hang over, but still he curls up like a baby. It is impossible to sleep and there is a light on in the corridor. So I sit here in my crib and write. I try to sort out what has happened.

Later

This is why I am mad at Miss Liberty. It was because of her I got the cinder in my eye that turned it red, which made the doctors think I have this terrible eye disease, trachoma. When our ship came into the harbor of New York everyone crowded at the rails to see the famous Statue of Liberty. I could not see because everyone was pushing in front of me. I am short, so I begged Papa to please hold me up. Just at that minute when he hoisted me onto his shoulder — well, it was as if that old lady Liberty spit in my eye. A cinder flew right into it. I knew everyone said it was from the smokestack of the ship, but it came directly from that spiky crown that stupid statue wears on her head. What is she doing wearing a crown anyhow? They are not supposed to have kings and queens here in America.

So when we arrive at Ellis Island and we are waiting for the medical doctors to examine us I do everything Mama says. For example, there is a long staircase which we had to climb to the examination room. Mama said, "Step lively. They look for people who are weak and lame on these stairs." So I stepped lively. We hear stories about how people are sent back if they seem unhealthy or "wrong," as Mama says, in some way. We go into the examination room. All is fine with the doctors until one comes with this funny little hook to flip up our eyelids. When it is my turn he flips up one lid and then the other. On the second lid he snorts. Just snorts and makes some letters with blue chalk on my back. All I remember then is Mama and Papa gasping and crying out. Before I knew it the door slams and I can still hear Mama crying on the other side. Must stop — nurse is coming. She has a nasty look. "Bedtime," she screeches.

Not bedtime — can't sleep

I am thinking all the time how this is like a nightmare come true. When we were at sea we were struck by a terrible storm a week out of Genoa. No one was allowed on deck. The ship creaked and moaned and every time it smacked down between the waves I swore it would break in two and I imagined drowning. Gabriella and Luca and I talked how if indeed the ship began to sink we would all hold hands. We would never let go of each other's hands no matter how hard the sea tore at us. We would go to the very bottom together. We would drown and die together wrapped in each other's arms. I thought until now drowning was the worst thing I could imagine. But this, this quarantine is worse. It is another kind of death, I think, and I hold no one's hand and no one holds mine. There are no arms to wrap me tight. I am completely and utterly alone. To be so alone and to have no one to tell you where your family is or if you will ever see them again is indeed a kind of death. I am sleepy now, but they never turn off the lights in the hallway. I see squiggles under my eyelids if I close them. Hard to sleep.

February 9, 1903

Tortellini dreams. Yes, I dream of tortellini. The food here is terrible. The people must have leather for tongues. Everything is tough, even the cooked cereal. It bounces against the spoon like rubber and everything has the taste of the cooking pots — like metal.

So I dream my tortellini dreams. Mama made the best tortellini. She filled the little dough rings with three different kinds of cheeses and mixed in little specks of fresh basil. Then she folded them just so. Mama's tortellini looked like — yes, I know it sounds odd — belly buttons. But they did. They were little lopsided rings with the top part flopped over a bit. When Mama wasn't looking, Luca and I would slip them onto our fingers and then slide them off into our mouths. It is the best way to eat tortellini. But if Mama caught us doing that she'd give our ears a twist and scold us.

I remember my tomato dreams. They seem like years ago, although it was only a few days ago that I dreamed of Miss Liberty with a tomato stuck on her torch. You know what I would do with that tomato now? I'd smash it right in her big fat face!

It all seems so long ago. Giuseppe and Gabriella holding hands. Signora Salami — I almost miss her! Franco and the bell-ringing turning my brain topsy-turvy. All so long ago!

Later

My first decent food. I never would have guessed something so strange could taste so good. It is yellow and curved. It has a very thick skin which you must peel off, although the old man next to me did not. He tried to eat it with the skin on. And the nurse, the one with the awful scolding voice, yelled at him and snatched it away. She peeled it and then shoved it at him. She said a word, an English word, "idiot." I do not think that is his name, because when the doctors come they call him something else. It sounds like "Joe." The doctors come to see me, too. They are very stern faced. They know I do not speak English so they never say anything to me or look me in the eye. I might as well be a vegetable they are looking at. One of the doctors has a bald head except for three long thick strands of hair that he combs over the top. They look like oily worms crawling across his skull. There are so far no children my age.

February 10, 1903

So far, I said! But now there is one. Someone my age. Yes, a girl! At first I thought she was the oddest creature I had ever seen. No wonder she is in quarantine! She must have some terrible illness to turn her hair that color red. And her skin is so pale that she is nearly transparent except for her freckles.

I first saw her after supper standing in the shadows of the corridor. She was trembling and so white, except for her hair. She reminded me of a small lick of fire, like the quivering flame on a guttering candle. But I was drawn to that flame like a moth on a summer's night. I just felt my feet walking a straight line to her. I stopped a foot, no more, in front of her. We both stood silently staring into one another's face. And then — I cannot quite explain it — her voice came like a song, a bird song. It floated out of her all silvery and musical. And I understood her perfectly — like magic! "My name is Maureen O'Malley," she said.

So I say back to her, "My name is Sofia Monari."

"I am from Ireland," she says.

"I am from Italy," I say.

"I am in quarantine," she says.

"I am in quarantine," I say.

She points to her eye and begins to speak rapidly. I do not understand all she says now, but one word is clear — "trachoma." And I begin speaking fast in Italian and some bits of English. Then she raises her hand to her hair and sticks out her fingers like spokes. Instantly I know what she means. Miss Liberty! That cursed statue. We both hate her! And now I know the English word. It is "cinder." Yes, *brace* is "cinder" in English. We are, Maureen and I, fast friends. We are united in these United States of America by our anger at Miss Liberty. What an awful woman to cause cinders to blow in our eyes just because we wanted to see her.

Later

A nurse, not the mean one, led us to two new beds. No more cribs. Maureen and I shall sleep side by side. I do not know where poor Mr. Joe is. But all that is important now is that I have a friend. We whisper Italian and English words in the night. But then I say, "No Italian. I learn English." Then Maureen says, and I understand every word, "I am your English teacher. Goodnight, Sofia."

And I say, "I am your English student."

And Maureen says, "I am your friend, Sofia."

And I say, "I am your friend, Maureen."

February 11, 1903

I decided this morning that Maureen and I must find the old man, Mr. Joe. I worry about him. Before we were moved, they came around with bananas again. The mean nurse snatched his away and said something. I think it meant, "He's too stupid to know how to eat this." But then I grabbed it from her. She was surprised. I began peeling it for Mr. Joe. She said one very sharp word — "fresh." I don't know what it means. But this is why I worry about Mr. Joe. That mean nurse is no good for him. I explain all this the best I can to Maureen. It is amazing how much Maureen and I can understand each other. Here is what I have already learned about her:

She has fourteen sisters and brothers.

She is number eleven.

Many are married, two are priests, one is a nun.

Only four came here with her parents to America.

Their names are Declan, Malachy, and Bridgid. (Strangest names I've ever heard.)

She comes from the village of Killcarrick, in what she calls County Clare. It is always rainy and foggy and there is much mud.

I have also told her about my family. "Cento"

sounds so much nicer than "Killcarrick." I told her about the tomatoes and the sunshine and the grape arbor at our back door. Here are some new English words I have learned: "sunny," "village," "mud," "fog," "brother," "sister," "priest," "nun." And now I can count to one hundred in English. That is good.

Later

We found Mr. Joe, and just in time. Mean Nurse was yelling at him and about to slap him because he spilled some applesauce. Maureen was on that nurse like a scalded cat. I could not understand her English, not one word — she spat them out so fast. She was shaking her finger. Imagine shaking your finger at a grown-up. Her face had turned as red as her hair. She didn't look like a guttering candle anymore. She looked like a raging bonfire. Then Nice

Nurse came over and asked Mean Nurse what was going on. I heard Mean Nurse say that word "fresh" again. Maureen began explaining things to Nice Nurse, this time more slowly. I caught several words. Then Nice Nurse got a sponge and began cleaning up Mr. Joe. She sent us to get more applesauce. Meanwhile, as all this was going on, I noticed a shadow slide by and someone small scramble away under Mr. Joe's bed. When I looked I saw something wrapped in foil under the bed. I unwrapped it. Chocolate! We divided it among the three of us. Nice Nurse didn't want any. Then Maureen and I said we would help feed Mr. Joe his applesauce, so we did. It would have been like playing dolls except that he's an old man. He has no teeth. His mouth caves in. His chin curls up and his long beak of a nose curves down and almost meets his chin. His face is shriveled and shrunken. It reminds me of a wrinkled apple.

February 12, 1903

At eleven o'clock every morning just after the snack cart passes through the nurses have coffee in their special alcove. All of a sudden today there was a terrible shriek. Mean Nurse jumped up screaming, "A mouse! A mouse! In my coffee cup!" Maureen and I raced over to see. There certainly was a little dead mouse curled up in the bottom of her coffee cup. Outside the alcove window I saw a blurred face, for the glass was smeared with soot. The face was laughing, I could tell. I nudged Maureen — "The Shadow," I whispered. I am sure the same person who left the chocolate put that mouse in Mean Nurse's cup.

The doctors will come this afternoon to check our eyes. Maureen is going to explain to them about Miss Liberty, the cinder and all of that. She is rehearsing her speech with me. I think it sounds lovely, but what do I know? Well, as of today nearly one hundred words in English. Good, but not good enough to explain to the doctors. So I hope Maureen's speech works.

February 13, 1903

Maureen's speech did not work. The doctors just stood there looking bored and impatient. "Old Worms" — that is what Maureen and I nicknamed the bald one with the disgusting hair strands — said something that made Maureen mad. She started spitting fire again, but she spoke slowly. "Are you calling me a liar?" she said.

"My, my! Aren't we fresh," said Old Worms. As soon as they left I asked Maureen what is "fresh." She explained. We have a word for it in Italian. It's what your mother smacks you up for when you are rude and impertinent. My mother, though, is not much of a smacker. Fresh isn't so bad, really. It is the easiest thing to talk about in the confession booth. "Bless me, Father, for I have sinned. I was fresh to my teacher." Four Hail Marys and a couple of Our Fathers usually takes care of it.

Later

Maureen and I go for a stroll after the doctors leave. We are both almost crying. You see, everything is so awful. No one tells us anything about how long we must stay here. Is it for another week? A month? A year? What about our mothers and fathers? I think of baby

Marco all the time. He might be crawling now and maybe even pulling himself up to stand. I so wanted to see Marco take his first step. But this is the worst thought of all. I dare not speak it aloud, but I do wonder if Maureen has had the same thought. What if Mama and Papa forget me? What if I just fade away in their minds?

Just after midnight

I am writing this in complete darkness, but the Shadow has come again! I was awakened by a rustling sound. Then I spied a bright, beautiful orange on my blanket and one on Maureen's, too. We have just finished eating them in the dark. We vow that tomorrow we shall find the Shadow.

February 14, 1903

What a strange place America is. In Italy and in Ireland people often go to a special mass on St. Valentine's Day. But here they send heart-shaped cards and sweets. We know this because Nice Nurse — we know her name now, Nancy — invited us to her special office for tea and cookies. She gave each of us a valentine. She said that she had some paper and colored pencils that we could use to make one for Mr. Joe. So we did.

Later

We gave Mr. Joe his valentine. Nancy said we could take him for a walk outside on the paved path, so we did. Mr. Joe speaks very few words of a language no one seems to understand.

Nancy says she thinks it's Croatian, which is what they speak in Austro-Hungary. He does understand when we say, "Come this way, Mr. Joe," and take his hand. Such happiness floods his face then. I keep thinking of Marco because I don't think Mr. Joe knows much more than a baby. But with Marco there is a light in his eyes. It is as if Marco dreams of what's to come — walking, playing, being a rascal. With Mr. Joe there is no light. There is no future in his eyes. It is as if he has been imprisoned forever in this dim, dreamless world of his brain which does not work quite right.

P.S. We have made no progress in tracking down the Shadow.

February 15, 1903

When we were outside on the paved walk yesterday we noticed a woman with hair an even a stranger color of red than Maureen's and very frizzy. She was looking out across the water clutching a handkerchief. I think she was crying. I could see a quiver ripple up her very straight back like a sob being stifled. Well, this morning we met her. She was having a very loud argument through an interpreter with the doctors in French — we think French. Suddenly she pulls off her frizzy hair and throws it at the doctor. It was a wig! Then Mean Nurse races up with another nurse and they put straps on her arms and pull her down into a wheelchair. It was horrid. "Let's get Nancy!" Maureen said. We ran off and Mean Nurse started yelling at us. We finally found Nancy and Maureen did the talking.

"Straps!" Nancy exploded ("straps" is my one hundred and fiftieth English word — sad word). "Restraints are against the rules. Wait until Chief hears about this!"

When we got back to the lady she was in the wheelchair but no straps. Her wig was back on her head, slightly crooked over one eyebrow. She began jabbering away but none of us understood her. I must have muttered something in Italian for all of a sudden she said in the clearest Italian, "Little one, I speak your language. Once I was engaged to Count Brandolini." Then she began speaking so fast I could heardly keep up even though it was Italian. But this is her story.

She calls herself Mademoiselle Coco. In Paris she was a seamstress. She sewed costumes for a famous dancing show called the Folies Bergère. Lots of feathers and glittering jewels on the costumes. She has come here because her heart was broken for "one last time." So she wanted to leave Paris. The doctors think she is sick because she wears a wig. Many people in Paris wear wigs, she says. But the reason she is wearing one is that her hair dresser burned her scalp with dye. Then she says the strangest thing of all. "The doctors say if I am bald no one will marry me. If I do not marry I shall not be able to support myself and the United States will have to support me. I have never been married and I have always made my own way! The government of France never paid me a cent," she shouts angrily. I am translating as best I can for Nancy and Maureen. Then Maureen says, "Ask her how she got her wig back and the straps off." So I do.

"A little boy," she says. "A dark little boy — a gypsy boy, I think."

The Shadow!

Later

Maureen and I are so excited because Mademoiselle Coco says he promised to come back! Nancy is not so interested in who took off the straps as much as who put them on. Then she asks if she might examine her scalp and Mademoiselle says yes. We ask Nancy if Mademoiselle Coco could sleep in the new empty bed on our ward. Nancy says that is fine.

February 16, 1903

The sky was just pulling back its night skin and the world was turning gray. I am not sure whether I heard soft voices first or smelled something like flowers. My eyes flew open and I saw Mademoiselle Coco sitting up in bed. She had on her wig, lip rouge, and thin eyebrows, which she did not have before, and was dabbing something the color of a sunset in a beautiful bottle on her neck. Perfume!

"Ah, my little one!" she says to me.

"Who were you talking to?" I ask.

She puts her finger to her mouth and then points down. At first I don't understand. Then I see those eyes — huge, black, shining with glints the way starlight floats on a still, black sea. A flash of dazzling white cracks the face. "Good morning, Sofia." He says this in a strange kind of Italian. "The Shadow!" I whisper.

"Why are you calling Rafi 'the Shadow,' little one?" Mademoiselle Coco asks.

I am so excited that I nearly forget to wake up Maureen. Luckily this ward is L-shaped. We are in the short arm of the L that only has our three beds. So we have more privacy. We bombard Rafi with questions. Rafi speaks a little of half a dozen languages. Rafi is a gypsy, and that is why he is here. "They no like the gypsies," he says.

"And they no like stowaways," Mademoiselle adds. We can't believe it. Rafi stowed away on a ship from Marseilles. He is an orphan. He's been on Ellis Island for three weeks. And this is the most fantastic: He was officially here and assigned a bed, but after two days he "disappeared." They thought he had fallen off the island and drowned. So they stopped looking for him. He is figuring out a plan to escape.

"But where will you go?" Maureen asks. "You're an orphan. No mother, no dad."

"I am a gypsy," he says, as if Maureen and I are the densest creatures on God's earth.

And he did bring the chocolate, the oranges, and the perfume for Mademoiselle, and the mouse and dog doo for Bad Nurse.

"But how do you get hold of such goodies — except the mouse and the dog doo, of course?" Maureen asks.

"How do you think? I am a gypsy." He humps up his shoulders and turns his palms to the ceiling as if to say, "It's as simple as that."

This could be the most exciting night of my life — or day, as it is morning now. Mademoiselle gave Maureen and me each a dab of perfume, so I imagine flowers as I close my eyes.

February 17, 1903

Maureen will eat anything. They fed us something for supper today that tasted like wet rags. I couldn't even touch it. What's more we are supposed to meet Rafi outside this evening, but Maureen is taking forever to eat. Rafi is going to lead us on what he calls a "tour." Going to show us things we won't believe. Perhaps a mountain of chocolate, or oranges. I don't know where he gets these goodies. Anyhow, Maureen keeps eating and eating and asking for seconds. Mademoiselle Coco thought it tasted awful, too. I didn't even know what it was — something they call "hash." Maureen says it's chopped-up potatoes with salt beef.

We had an argument. I said, "This is not a potato." Maureen said it was. She claims she is an expert in potatoes. I say never. This is like no potato I ever ate. I try to explain gnocchi to her which also has chopped up potatoes — Mama's potato gnocchi. They are little dumplings that dance on your tongue. You hardly need to chew them. They melt in your mouth. Meanwhile, Maureen is chomping and grinding her way through this hash. Poor Mr. Joe can hardly eat his. I pour tea into it and mash it up for him. It is my belief that if you have never tasted anything good you don't know what is bad. Would you believe that Maureen has never tasted a tomato? Didn't even know what one was, nor a tortellini. I had to draw a picture of both with the colored pencils that Nancy gave us for Valentine's Day. I made such a lovely tomato drawing. It rises like a big red sun in a field, and behind the huge red tomato you see the lovely rolling fields and hills of Cento. Then I made church spires in the background. "Oh, that does look good enough to eat," said Maureen. And, if I know Maureen, she might eat the paper and think it just fine!

February 18, 1903
Just after daybreak

Rafi knows everything about this place. We sneaked out this evening. For the first time since arriving at the hospital we went back over the bridge that connects the hospital with Ellis Island. There are a lot of "crooks" —

that is what Rafi calls them — who work on Ellis Island, he says. Money changers, dishonest inspectors who take bribes, baggage helpers who steal. Rafi says there is a gang of shipping inspectors who regularly steal right out of the cargo holds of ships, and they hide what they steal in the trash bins. So he took us to the trash bins and showed us where the crooks stash their stolen goods — sometimes under piles of garbage. He explained that the garbage collectors are in on the "swindle."

Rafi explains in a mixture of funny-sounding Italian and English: "You see, there's a system here. All these trash bins have a label with the letter *B* on them. *B* for Battery. The Battery is the part of the island of Manhattan at the very bottom of the island. It is just across from Ellis Island. The bins get taken to the Battery. That's where the fences come to get the stolen goods."

"A fence?" Maureen asks.

"People who sell stolen things." He took a lid off one trash can, reached in through the smelly garbage, and pulled out a bottle of whiskey. He reached in again and pulled out an expensive man's hat from a box. He set it on his head tipped over one eye. "Somewhere in one of these bins is a gold-handled walking cane. I'd make quite the gent, wouldn't I? Ah, here it is." Rafi began strutting up and down in front of the trash cans just as cocky as could be.

"How'd you learn all that stylishness?" Maureen asked.

"Oh, I've been in all the great cities of the world. London, Rome, Paris, Vienna. I know how they walk, how they talk."

He stopped in front of another can and took off the lid with a flourish. Extending his arm like a merchant in the finest store, he said, "Can I interest you ladies in anything? Take what you want. Here, we got watches." He held up a beautiful small gold watch with Roman numerals. It was delicate and on its face was a scroll of flowers. A lady's watch. I have never seen anything so pretty. "Here we got some nice silk stockings and shawls and here a very nice man's waistcoat." Rafi actually crawls into one trash bin and then from the trash his arm shoots up waving a fine leather belt. His huge dark eyes with their starry glints shine gleefully just over the rim of the trash bin. His teeth flash white. "See, some of these bins are big enough for people. Fine way to travel." He climbs out. "Over here — wine, whiskey, cheese." My stomach lurches. I sniff. Asiago! My favorite cheese. "Take something!" Maureen and I look at each other. We both have the same thought. "Bless me, Father, for I have sinned . . ."

"Come on," Rafi says. "You are only stealing from the stealers."

"Does that make us double thieves?" Maureen says. I am suddenly understanding too much English. Rafi takes two bars wrapped in foil. It is chocolate. I can smell it. "Take it." I feel my hand fold over it. I don't even want it. I want the cheese. I want Mama. I want to be out of here.

February 19, 1903

We went back to our hospital beds before dawn broke and crawled in so no one would miss us at morning check. I dreamed my tortellini dreams at first, but then they changed. I was in the pasta factory near Bologna where my uncle Gian Carlo is the supervisor. I see all the machines into which the dough goes and then squirts out the different noodles — fusilli, zitoni, linguine. Suddenly that huge factory room turns into the registry room here at Ellis Island. Instead of dough being turned into noodles it is immigrants being turned into Americans. We are all in the long lines again. Me, Mama, Papa, Gabriella, Marco, Luca. We shall go through this machine and be twisted and squeezed and come out Americans — except for me. The door slams. I scream.

When I opened my eyes Mademoiselle Coco was shaking me. "Wake up! wake up!"

I said, "Oh, it was just a bad dream."

"No, this is real. Quick, come to Mr. Joe," she cried.

February 20, 1903

Oh my goodness, so much has happened. None of it good. I arrived at Mr. Joe's bedside to see Mean Nurse shouting at him. She is holding that stupid chocolate bar. I didn't want all of it, so I gave half of mine to Mr. Joe. Mean Nurse is yelling, "Where did you get this? Where?" She is accusing him of stealing!

Mr. Joe, who can hardly feed himself, is just curled up mewling like a sick little kitty. Maureen ran all over to find Nancy but she is not at work today. We don't know anyone else to go to for help. We tried to get one young nurse but all she did was say, "Oh, we don't cross Miss Barron." I guess that is Mean Nurse's name.

Finally we found one of the doctors who checked our eyes. But as soon as he came Mean Nurse turned sweet as honey. Started dabbing Mr. Joe's mouth with a damp cloth, smoothing his blankets, cooing to him and calling him sweet names. "I thought you girls said there was a problem," the doctor said.

"There are a million problems!" Maureen exploded. And then she begins telling him how Mean Nurse was yelling at poor Mr. Joe just because of some dumb chocolate bar. And Mean Nurse denies the whole thing. She just says, "Oh, these girls get such fancies in their heads."

I don't know what the word "fancies" means exactly, but I think it is something to do with "lie." The next thing I know, Maureen is yelling, "Are you calling us liars?" A strange look came over Mean Nurse's face, but just for a second. There was something very deadly about it. Then she smiled, not a nice smile at all, and in the pit of my stomach I felt a darkness. A coldness began to creep up and flood into my veins. I knew in that instant that Mean Nurse would never let us off this island. I knew she was determined to do something terrible to Maureen and me. We must both be very careful now. I think we must meet with Rafi soon. He will know what to do. And much more needs to be done than putting a mouse in Mean Nurse's coffee cup.

Later

Mouse in a coffee cup! What about what Mean Nurse is putting into our glasses of milk? This afternoon Mademoiselle Coco saw Mean Nurse put some kind of powder in two glasses of milk on the snack cart. We are the last ones to get the snack cart as we are in the short end of the L-shaped ward. Mademoiselle was coming back from the bathroom and saw her. She managed to bump into Mean Nurse just as

Mean Nurse was handing us our glasses of milk. So they spilled and broke. Mean Nurse was furious but ran quickly to get some more. That is when Mademoiselle told us about the powder. This is really getting scary. Is she trying to poison us? I can't wait until Nancy comes back on duty tomorrow.

February 21, 1903

No Nancy! She is out sick. No sign of Rafi, either. Mademoiselle borrowed my colored pencils and drew pictures of the costumes she used to design for the Folies Bergère. They were beautiful, lots of ruffles on skirts. She showed pictures of the dancers kicking up their legs. She explained how she had to design the skirts so they would be very light and float up in the air to show the dancers' garters! We drew for an hour or more. I drew pictures of tomatoes and one of our house in Cento and our chicken yard. Mademoiselle says I am a talented artist.

But what does it all mean? We're stuck here on this awful island. Maureen and I feel utterly hopeless. No one understands us. The doctors come by and peer into our eyes and say, "Let's wait and see."

I want to say, "Let's wait and see what? Let's wait and see if Marco is all grown up by the time you let me out of here? That Mama and Papa have gray hair? That Gabriella is married? That Luca is . . ." I don't know what.

That is the problem. I know nothing of my family and they know nothing of me. An ocean might as well separate us. I cannot believe this is really happening. I cannot believe these people, these doctors are real human beings. I am even getting mad at Nancy. Doesn't anyone believe that we are children? That we belong with our families? I think half the time that this is a terrible nightmare. But I never seem to wake up from it. And then sometimes I think it is a terrible game and maybe I am just not clever enough for it. One thing is for sure. Maureen and I have vowed never to take milk from the snack cart. And we are very careful about what we eat.

February 23, 1903

A signal from Rafi this evening. A bit of foil just like that found on the chocolate and a clock face with the hands drawn on at a quarter before midnight. That is almost when the new shift of nurses comes on. Maureen and I talk with Mademoiselle. She knows all about our going to the trash bins with Rafi. She says that the drawing of the clock is a sign for us to meet him there at fifteen minutes before midnight. She says we should go. If any nurses come to check she will figure out an excuse.

Mademoiselle is sad these days. She fears that she will have to wait to get out until all her hair grows back. She has spent most of her time writing letters — letters to the French embassy in America and letters to important people in France. During the day she is full of hope and good cheer. She seems all bright and sparkly. Her hair, even though it is a wig, glows, her eyes shine, but at night she seems to grow dim. She says very sad things like, "Who has use for an old woman?" Or, "What is left for an old woman like me? Memories? We must live just on memories, not even good food here. I shall die."

Maureen and I try to cheer her up. But tonight none of us has the will for some reason. We shall stay awake until it is time to go see Rafi. At least maybe we can bring Mademoiselle back some perfume. She loves perfume. I don't care about stealing anymore. I don't care about sin. "Father, bless me, for I have sinned?" No. *They* have sinned. The doctors, the nurses, the inspectors who keep us here. Father, bless me, and get me out of here!

February 24, 1903

Just back from meeting Rafi. This time we hid in the shadows of the chimneys near the trash bins. And do you know what we saw in the dead of night? The cheats. The swindlers. All the people who make money off the belongings taken from the immigrants. I saw the guard who stood at the steps as we walked up that long flight where mother told us to step lively. I know it was him. Who was next to him? The buttonhook doctor who first flipped my eyelid open! Then there were others I could not see, but their long shadows crisscrossed the pavement. I heard their voices. Men and women. "Oh, I think I'll keep this one for myself, Jimmy." It was a woman's voice, and then she added, "But here's another. How much do you think these will fetch?"

Rafi mouthed two words that I didn't understand. Then in a low whisper after they had gone he explained those words — "thieves market." It is a market for stolen goods. Goods stolen from immigrants.

February 25, 1903

"You are stealing me! You are stealing me!" I wake up and Mademoiselle Coco is leaning over me. "What are you saying? No one is stealing you. You are here in your bed between Maureen and me. Safe in your bed." I open my eyes and realize that I have been dreaming, but this dream is real. I am not safe in my bed at all. The truth hits me. We are all goods, damaged goods on some awful thieves market. Our lives are not our own. Our lives do not even belong to the parents who gave birth to us.

"What's wrong, dear?" It is Nancy. She sits down at the foot of my bed. She is finally back. But now I look at her with new eyes. She is part of it all. An ugly grown-up game to keep us from our parents, from America. If she really cared about us why wouldn't she get us out? I glare at her and refuse to answer. She comes up and puts her hand on my forehead to check for fever. "No fever," she says quickly. No, I think, but inside I am boiling. Something is going to happen. I cannot bear this. Just then a sharp voice cuts through. "Bed 33. No breathing."

I roll over and hide my head under the pillow. Bed 33. That is Mr. Joe!

Later

Mr. Joe has had a heart attack. He is having trouble breathing. Maureen and I sit, one on each side of him, holding his hands. We speak to him softly. I mostly speak in Italian. I don't think it matters if he understands the exact words. He knows, I think, that we are here. His eyes are not really open but not all the way shut. I can see the white part through the slit. I think his eyes have rolled back into his head. I have many odd thoughts as I look at him. I wonder if he is close to God now. If God is whispering in his ear. I wonder if he can understand.

I think you can always understand God.

Brains don't really matter for that. I begin to look at Mr. Joe very carefully. His skin does not look so wrinkled to me. I can almost imagine what he looked like as a young man, maybe even as a young boy. And his hands, even though his fingernails are yellow and split and dirty and his knuckles swollen, are nice hands with very long fingers. They say that the great artist Michelangelo had beautiful, long, strong hands. They must have been special hands to form the shapes from the blocks of marble. Mama has a picture postcard of the *David* statue in Florence and then the paintings on the ceilings of the Sistine Chapel. I look at Mr. Joe's hands and I think what those hands could have made, had this poor man's brain worked properly. I look at my hands. I nearly laugh. They draw good tomatoes. Tomatoes that Maureen says she could eat right off the paper. What a funny thought. I stifle a giggle. How odd to have such funny thoughts at this terrible time. Sometimes Mr. Joe seems to forget to breathe. Maureen and I watch for his chest to rise and it doesn't. So we nudge him a bit and then he begins to breathe. We vow we shall stay here all night. We shall not leave Mr. Joe alone. He must not die alone and in the dark in this terrible place.

February 26, 1903

We have stayed all night with Mr. Joe. Sometimes we dozed. We took turns, really, but one of us was always awake. In the darkest hours, when no one was around, Rafi came. He slipped a rosary into Mr. Joe's hands. Maureen mouthed the words, "The trash bins?" Rafi nodded. Imagine this place where they even put crucifixes on the thieves market. I laced the beads of the crucifix chain through

Mr. Joe's fingers and again thought how truly lovely those hands were. Suddenly another hand was there, taking his pulse. On the wrist of that hand was a slender gold watch with roman numerals and a face inscribed with flowers. A chill ran through me. I looked up. It was Mean Nurse. She gave a quick, brittle smile. "Nice of you girls to be here." I was too stunned to speak or even nod. She said something about a woman having a baby. Then a few minutes later we saw a lady heavy with child being helped into a bed just down the corridor and curtains being drawn around the bed.

Later

Nancy comes and begs us to go to her office with her for some tea and cookies. But we won't. Nancy knows there is something wrong with us more than Mr. Joe's being sick. Maureen saw the watch, too. We cannot trust anybody. The doctors come by. They compliment us for staying by Mr. Joe. But their words have no meaning. Can't they see that this is not the place where we should be? We should be with our families. Have these men no families?

Later

This is a strange hour. We are near midnight. The pregnant lady down the corridor groans. I guess it is coming time for her to give birth. What a place to be born! And while this baby is pushing into this ugly world Mr. Joe's pulse is getting weaker. His face, however, seems younger. I noticed it and then Maureen said, "Look, can't you almost imagine Mr. Joe as a boy?" So that is exactly what we do. We begin imagining Mr. Joe as a boy, in a country whose name we do not know, with a language we have hardly heard him speak.

Maureen beings by saying, "I can see you, Mr. Joe, on a haystack, sliding down with pieces of hay sticking out from your hair. You have thick blond hair. I think you are very daring because you can climb the highest haystack and jump down and land on your feet."

Then I begin. I speak a mixture of Italian and English. But I tell Mr. Joe a story about how he caught a trout in a bubbling stream. It was a huge one with a pink throat and lovely green speckles on its sides. He brought it home and his mother stuffed it with mushrooms and made a fragrant tomato and basil sauce. And then we begin a story about how Mr. Joe on a frosty night sneaked out of his bedroom window to meet a pretty girl. They met at a pond where they went skating and they kissed in the moonlight.

Oh, that was the best one of all. Maureen and I got so carried away with the skating and the sound of the blades on the ice and the moonlight that we did not even notice that Mr. Joe had slipped away. He simply died and there was the nicest look on his face. Maybe he is skating to heaven.

Later

It is so odd. Maureen and I are not really sad. We are instead filled with a strange kind of joy. I said a little prayer asking that in heaven Mr. Joe might become a boy once more with a brain that works right. Yes, I surely believe this will happen. That will be heaven for Mr. Joe. And in spite of all the terrible things that happened to Mr. Joe here on earth and the mean things here on Ellis Island I really do believe that sooner or later God does look out for us.

February 27, 1903

The little baby was born this afternoon. A girl, but she didn't live more than an hour. "Lucky," Maureen whispered. The mother was a gypsy, and from what Rafi tells us about how the inspectors treat gypsies, the mother and baby might never have been let into the country. Maureen and I can't figure out why Rafi ever came here if they are so against gypsies. But Rafi says everyone is against gypsies. He never tells us much about where he came from or anything about his family. We have no idea if he has any brothers or sisters. Maybe this makes it easy for him. No one to miss. It is almost as if Rafi were born all grown up.

Later

This is unbelievable. Maureen and I are being forced to see another doctor. A doctor who "just talks" to us about the thoughts in our head. Mean Nurse overheard us say "lucky" when the baby died. So now they think there is something wrong with our brains. This is very bad. If they decide we are feebleminded or something we shall be sent away to a crazy house or back to our home countries. Then we shall never see our parents again. Nancy came to us this morning and said, "Did you really say that about the baby?" I was about to shake my head no. I was going to lie. I have decided that lying in a place like this doesn't count. But Maureen wouldn't be quiet. "Of course we said that. Why would anybody want to be born in this place? Especially a gypsy baby? Everything is upside down here." Then Maureen said something I couldn't believe. "And you're no better, Nancy. Oh yes, you give us cookies in your little office and colored pencils for us to amuse ourselves with. But what have you really done to help us get to our families? We know nothing of them, and for all we know they know nothing of us."

I cannot believe that Maureen said all this. Nancy's face just turned white and her lower lip began to tremble. She turned on her heel and almost ran away.

Later

The weather has turned warm. Maureen and I go out on the paved promenade that encircles the whole island. From a small rise we can see the ferryboats arriving with the new immigrants. We watch them stream off the gangplanks and up the ramps leading into the "factory." Yes, that is how I think of Ellis Island now. Even though the main building with its fancy brick-and-stone-trimmed towers, its cupolas and spires, looks like a palace, it is nothing but a factory that turns immigrant lumps of dough into Americans — except, of course, for me and Maureen, Mr. Joe and Mademoiselle Coco, and gypsies.

February 28, 1903

So far we have not been taken to see the doctor for our heads. The weather is still warm and Mademoiselle Coco, Maureen, and I continue to take walks outside. We have not seen Rafi for two days. No chocolates, no perfume. A few blades of grass poke through the hard, bare ground. But there are not many trees. I see leaf buds on some branches of these few trees but I wonder how the leaves will hang on for everything here is so scrubbed by the wind. A barge is just pulling away. It is loaded with trash bins. It looks as if it is heading for Manhattan Island, so it must have the bins with the B for Battery, many loaded with fine goods stolen from the immigrants. When Mademoiselle and Maureen and I turn the corner and walk directly into the wind we must link arms to make any headway against it.

That was just how we were walking when suddenly I heard a voice very much like Maureen's. "Now what have we here? Three lovely ladies out for a stroll on a blustery day like this!" We were shocked. We had never met anyone on our walks. Since we are considered to have contagious diseases and we are outside the walls of the hospital there is a strict rule forbidding us to speak to anyone. We looked up. "Oh, Father," gasped Maureen. For indeed before us stood a Catholic priest. Tall with thick rusty-colored hair and webs of crinkled lines spreading out from the corners of his eyes. As handsome a man as there ever was. "What brings out such fine ladies . . . and on an island like this?" He looked about at the hospital, the dark chimneys poking at the sky. It was such an enormous question, really, one hardly knew where to begin. But I suddenly realized that this was a question that one put to people who were free and not imprisoned as we were.

"Oh, Father," Maureen said in a low voice. "You cannot speak to us."

"Must not or can not, dear? And do I detect the music of County Clare in your voice?"

"Yes, Father, you do, but you must not

speak to us. They say we have diseases that one could catch."

"How long have you been here, child?"

"Sofia and me, nearly three weeks here. Mademoiselle almost as long."

"And your parents?"

"We know nothing of them," I said in the best English I could. "The Golden Door slammed in our faces in the registry room and *pfft!*" I whipped the air with my hand to show how our parents disappeared from us and we from them.

Father's face bunched into a frown. "I know. I've seen too much of this in the few days that I've been here. That's why I've stayed."

"You mean," Maureen asked, "you've stayed here on purpose?"

"Yes, my dear. There are too many stories like yours, too much bribery. If they can't pay the bribe too many end up detained or, worse yet, 'excluded' and sent back to where they came from."

Then Father Finnegan, for that was his name, said that he was going "to see about things." He took out a piece of paper and wrote our names down and the number of beds in the hospital.

I have no idea what will happen. Mademoiselle Coco says not to count on anything.

March 1, 1903

Rafi is gone. We know this for certain. When we came back from our walk yesterday, under each of our pillows was a gift — a little gold bracelet for Maureen, a bottle of perfume for Mademoiselle, and for me a locket on a chain. When I opened the locket instead of a picture there was one single letter written in a very wobbly hand. *B*. This was his good-bye. Rafi was on the very barge that we saw pulling away as we were on our walk. And the *B* was for Battery, just like the *B* marked on the trash bins. That is exactly how Rafi left — in a trash bin — of this I am sure. I picture him sprinkled with wet coffee grounds, his thick dark hair laced with banana peels and gold chain watches. What will the fences think when he's pulled out?

March 2, 1903

Maureen and I begin to think of escaping like Rafi. We figure that we could both fit in one of those trash bins together. But the problem is how we would find our parents once we got to Manhattan. Maureen says we could go to a church, that the nuns would help us. I'm not so sure. You hear of nuns finding little babies on doorsteps all swaddled up. But we're really too big to be all bundled up and cooed over. I think they'd just turn us into nuns. Maureen says they can't turn you into a nun unless you want to be turned into one. But I say that we are just two nine-year-old girls and we shall be put down in the middle of New York City with millions of people. Dangerous things could happen. We could be kidnapped.

Maureen says, "Are you daft? We *are* kidnapped." She has a point. I wish that Father Finnegan would come around again. Tomorrow the head doctors want to see us. They still, I guess, have not forgotten that we said the baby was lucky to die. Nancy keeps trying to be nice to us. But, well, it is just hard. If she really wanted to help us, wouldn't she do something? She says she knows that we do not have trachoma. We asked her to try and find out about our parents. She says that she has been trying but there are papers that must be found. Because she is a nurse and not in the inspector's office she is not allowed to see them.

March 3, 1903

Nancy came in this morning and told us that Maureen's and my papers have somehow been lost! This means that there is no record of our families, their names, where they were going to live. Nancy is furious. And all Mean Nurse says is, "It happens sometimes." Nancy wants to call in a social worker for our cases but Mean Nurse says they are overloaded with work. Nancy and Mean Nurse are having a huge fight as I write this. I guess Nancy really is on our side. Now I hear Mean Nurse saying, "Well, it's time for their appointment anyhow."

"What appointment?" Nancy asks.

"They are going to be examined by Doctor Cochrane and Doctor Gilbert."

"Why in heaven's name?" asks Nancy.

"They threatened to kill that baby who died the other day."

"They what?" says Nancy. Before I know it, Maureen is flying at Mean Nurse. Her hands balled into fists, little Maureen hurls herself at Mean Nurse and they both crumple to the ground. Maureen is pummeling Mean Nurse with her fists and saying the worst words imaginable — at least I think, for I only understand a couple. She had whispered them to me at night when she described the bloody fights in her lane in Killcarrick between the Hanrahans and the O'Briens. Two men come and pull Maureen off Mean Nurse.

Later

"Are you often violent, Maureen? And what about you, Sofia?" The doctors asks. Well, we must look pretty violent, I guess. "Ruffian," that is what my uncle Gian Carlo would say about us. It was his expression for really bad tough fellows. Maureen is standing there with a bloody lip. My own petticoat is torn for I was down on the floor yelling my head off at Mean Nurse. Yes, I admit it, I did give her a whack. Mean Nurse is standing in the doctor's office with blood streaming out of her nose. I guess it will be jail for us, I am thinking. The nuns wouldn't have us on a silver platter with the relics of Saint Jude for trimmings. Saint Jude, by the way, is the saint for lost causes. That's Maureen and me. Lost causes.

"What about this baby you threatened to kill?"

"We did not threaten to kill the baby," Maureen says. Her voice is dead flat.

"You deny it?"

"Yes," Maureen says.

"And you, too, Sofia." I do not know what the word "deny" means, but I say yes. Then Nancy chimes in, "Of course they deny it, doctors."

"Please don't interrupt, Miss Burns."

"I think it is time to interrupt," says a voice from behind us. "Is this a medical examination or a court of law? Where are these girls' guardians? By what right do you have to haul them in here?"

"Who are you?"

"Father Finnegan, and I have recently contacted the archbishop of the Diocese of

New York as well as the commissioner general of Ellis Island, William Williams. He's a good man. He doesn't like to see corruption on his island, let alone innocent children separated from their parents for weeks on end and being treated like common criminals. How do you explain the loss of their papers? How do you explain that these girls do not appear to have a trace of the eye disease for which they have been detained? How do you explain that their parents have not been contacted? Would you not become violent, sirs, under such circumstances? Would you perhaps think if you saw a newborn baby die in this place that perhaps t'would be better to go to heaven and be cradled in the arms of the Almighty than those arms . . ." Father Finnegan paused and then turned slowly toward Mean Nurse. Mean Nurse looked at him as if she were about to hiss. "Miss Barron. Miss Lillian Barron. I believe that is your name?" She nodded warily. "And the lovely watch on your wrist, how did you come by that?"

"How dare you?"

"Well, how did you come by it?"

"My father gave it to me on the occasion of my twenty-first brithday."

"May I see it?"

"No!"

"Well, if I may not see it, would you prove to me that inscribed on the back of that watch are not these words." Father Finnegan drew from his pocket a scrap of paper. On it I saw letters wobbly just like the B that Rafi had made. "To my beloved wife Miriam on our thirtieth wedding anniversary, September 21, 1903 — Love, Harry."

"It's a lie."

"Prove it."

Father Finnegan held out his hand for the watch, but Lillian Barron fled.

The doctors were stunned. Maureen and I were stunned and Nancy stood with her mouth hanging open.

"This is an impressive amount of information you have gathered, Father," said Dr. Gilbert.

"And it is an impressive amount of information you have lost on these children, doctors. It is high time that children stop slipping through the cracks in the system here on Ellis Island, especially if you are a poor child and cannot afford the bribes to avoid having your coat chalked falsely, or maybe you're just a gypsy child." He paused and looked at Maureen and me. It was then that we knew that somehow, someway, Rafi had met with Father Finnegan before he packed himself into that trash can for the final leg of his journey to America.

March 5, 1903

So much has happened I don't know how I shall write it all down. Father Finnegan, through the ship's documents kept in the main office, found the names of our parents and the ships we had arrived on. Then today Nancy and Father Finnegan came in at three o'clock in the morning to wake us up.

Father also shook Mademoiselle. "What?" she says. "What?"

"Yes, Mademoiselle, you're going, too. Put on your wig."

We are all so excited. Nancy and Father Finnegan have brought extra coats for us, for outside there is a slashing, icy rain. They bundle us onto the little ferryboat that brings over the shifts of workers. Although it is a short trip the water is very choppy and the boat must go slowly, but finally we land at the pier. The lamplight is smudged in the swirl of rain and fog. But I see some figures huddled by a large gate. They are like one big bundle squashed against the grating of the gate.

"Malachy." The name tears from Maureen's throat. Then I see, like a bright little lamp shining out from the opening of a huge coat, a tiny chubby face. "Marco!"

Maureen and I race across the black slick pavement. We fling ourselves against the grating. I feel metal. I feel flesh. My cheek presses against the small portion of Mama's that pushes through the opening of the grate.

"Hold on! Hold on! We'll open the gate," a voice shouts. But we can hardly tear ourselves from the gate, from the touch of our own families' cheeks, noses. We do not even want an inch to separate us. But then at last we are in their arms. Maureen and I are home and free at last.

I shall never forget Father Finnegan. Some immigrants came through the Golden Door to America, some like Rafi came in a trash can. But Maureen and Mademoiselle Coco and I came tucked in the heart of one man.

Life in America
in 1903

Historical Note

Although Sofia Monari is a fictional character and although hers is not the usual story of immigrants coming to America, it is the story of those who were detained for a variety of reasons, some fairly and some unfairly, on Ellis Island.

Immigrants' first glimpse of Statue of Liberty from ship's deck

Ellis Island first opened as a station for arriving immigrants on New Year's Day, 1892. The number of immigrants had been rising

An immigrant family waiting at Ellis Island

steadily, and between 1880 and 1900 over nine million people had come to the United States, the largest number of new arrivals ever. Many Americans were frightened, for prior to this time most immigrants had come from northern and western European countries, mainly Scandinavia, Germany, Austria, England, and Ireland. But now people from Italy, Poland,

Spain, Greece, Austro-Hungary, Russia and Eastern Europe were pouring into America. They felt that these people were more "foreign," and shared less of what they considered their mutual Anglo background. Before Ellis Island, Castle Garden on the southern tip of Manhattan had handled immigration. However, in 1890 this facility became inadequate for the rising tide of immigration and thus Ellis Island was built in upper New York Bay, near the New

A view of Castle Garden

Jersey shore. Channels were dredged, the island itself enlarged, docks built, and buildings constructed, such as a hall for registration and inspection, a utility plant, a hospital, a laundry, and dormitories.

Five years after it opened in 1897 a fire broke out on Ellis Island and destroyed most of the buildings which were made of pine. But shortly after the fire, rebuilding started and these new buildings were made of brick. The new station opened in 1900. Every immigrant

Ellis Island in 1903

who passed through Ellis Island had interesting stories to tell. Many of America's

A family registers at Ellis Island

most illustrious people — doctors, writers, social activists, priests, musicians, sports stars — came to America through Ellis Island. Among them were Irving Berlin, a famous songwriter; Al Jolson, an actor and singer; Samuel Goldwyn, a film industry pioneer; Frank Capra, a movie director; Felix

Frankfurter, a Supreme Court judge; Knute Rockne, a football coach; Bob Hope, a comedian; and Father Flanagan, a priest and the founder of Boys Town.

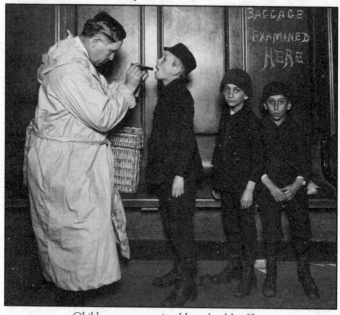

Children are examined by a health officer

One out of every five immigrants who passed through Ellis Island was held in detention or quarantine for health or other, often vague, reasons. There they were to be "processed," which meant that they met all the requirements to satisfy the officials for admission into the United States. Two percent of all the immigrants were excluded and sent back to the country from which they had come. The immigrants often encountered corrupt officials who were all too eager to make money off the newly arrived and innocent people through bribery, thievery, and the selling of forged citizenship papers.

Detained immigrants waiting

Eventually many of these problems were cleaned up, but a real prejudice persisted toward southern and eastern European people as well as gypsies.

Immigration began to decline in the 1920s, and during the Great Depression in the 1930s more people left America than entered. During World War II the island was used mostly as a detention center for enemy aliens — people from countries against which

Quarantine

the United States was fighting, such as Japan, Germany, and Italy. Ellis Island was formally closed on November 12, 1954, since there was no more need for an immigration station of that size. In 1965 President Lyndon Johnson declared the island a national monument to be administered, along with the Statue of Liberty, as part of the National Park Service under the Department of Interior. The buildings on Ellis Island had fallen into disrepair and restoration work began in 1983. Seven years later construction was finished and the exhibit halls completed. Ellis Island opened its doors in 1990 to its first visitors.

Millions of Americans today have ancestors who passed through the registry room of Ellis Island. The stories of these immigrants have inspired many people to search out their own family histories. For those people who wish to trace their relatives through Ellis Island there are many resources available that can help them in their search. It is important before one begins to have the names of any ancestors and where they came from. Dates are also important, such as those of birth, death, and marriage.

The Registry Room at Ellis Island

About the Author

Kathryn Lasky is the author of more than forty books for children and adults, including the second book of Sofia's Immigrant Diary, *Home At Last*. She has also written four books for the Dear America series: *A Journey to the New World*, *Dreams in the Golden Country*, *Christmas After All*, and *A Time for Courage*. She is also the author of Newbery Honor book *Sugaring Time*.

Acknowledgments

Grateful acknowledgment is made for permission to reprint the following:

Cover Portrait by Glenn Harrington

Page 95: Immigrants on ship's deck, Culver Pictures, New York.

Page 96: Immigrant family, North Wind Picture Archives, Alfred, Maine.

Page 97: Castle Garden, H. C. White/CORBIS, New York.

Page 98: Ellis Island, Courtesy of Ellis Island.

Page 99: Immigrants on Ellis Island, SuperStock, Jacksonville, Florida.

Page 100: Medical examination on Ellis Island, Bettmann/CORBIS, New York.

Page 101: Detained immigrants, North Wind Picture Archives, Alfred, Maine.

Page 102: Quarantine, CORBIS, New York.

Page 104: Ellis Island Registry Room, Getty Images, New York.

Other books in the My America series

Corey's Underground Railroad Diaries
by Sharon Dennis Wyeth

Elizabeth's Jamestown Colony Diaries
by Patricia Hermes

Hope's Revolutionary War Diaries
by Kristiana Gregory

Joshua's Oregon Trail Diaries
by Patricia Hermes

Meg's Prairie Diaries
by Kate McMullan

Sofia's Immigrant Diaries
by Kathryn Lasky

Virginia's Civil War Diaries
by Mary Pope Osborne

While the events described and some of the characters in this book
may be based on actual historical events and real people, Sofia
Monari is a fictional character, created by the author, and her diary
is a work of fiction.

Copyright © 2003 by Kathryn Lasky

Library of Congress Cataloging-in-Publication Data
Lasky, Kathryn.
Hope in my heart / by Kathryn Lasky.
p.   cm. — (My America) (Sofia's immigrant diary ; bk.1)
Summary: After her family immigrates to America from Italy in 1903, ten-year-old
Sofia is quarantined at the Ellis Island Immigration Station, where she makes a good
friend but endures nightmarish conditions. Includes historical notes.
ISBN 0-439-18875-X; 0-439-44962-6 (pbk.)
[1. Ellis Island Immigration Station (N.Y. and N.J.) — Juvenile fiction.   2. Ellis Island
Immigration Station (N.Y. and N.J.) — Fiction.   3. Immigrants — Fiction.   4. Italian
Americans — Fiction.   5. Diaries — Fiction.   6. United States — Emigration and
immigration — Fiction.   7. New York (N.Y.) — History — 1898–1951 — Fiction.]
I. Title.   II. Series.
PZ7.L3274 Hq 2003
[Fic] — dc21   2002044558
CIP   AC

10 9 8 7 6 5 4 3 2 1   03 04 05 06 07

The display type was set in Edwardian Medium.
The text type was set in Goudy.
Photo research by Amla Sanghvi.
Book design by Elizabeth B. Parisi.

Printed in the U.S.A.   23
First edition, November 2003